Praise for
My Mother's Wish

"An enchanted, stirring tale about the greatest and most surprising gifts, acceptance and love."

> —Elizabeth Dewberry, author of *His Lovely Wife,*
> *Sacrament of Lies,* and *Break the Heart of Me*

"Over the years I've read about every conceivable kind of Christmas story that existed. Then came this one: truly a wondrous one-of-a-kind tale bringing laughter and tears. If it were possible to fuse the writing styles and messages of Garrison Keillor, C. S. Lewis, Dave Barry, and Catherine Marshall, the result might very well bear the title *My Mother's Wish*."

> —JOE L. WHEELER, PHD, editor of the Christmas
> in My Heart® story anthology series

"Jerry Camery-Hoggatt explores the mystical relationship that binds mothers and children together and gives all of us an opportunity to revisit that magical time as our own mothers dragged us, kicking and screaming at times, through childhood. This is a book that makes you think—and remember. You will want to call and thank your own mother and tell her you love her."

—ED BUTCHART, professional and official Santa, Stone Mountain, Georgia, and author of *The Red Suit Diaries* and *More Pages from the Red Suit Diaries*

"Eleanor Crumb McKutcheon—call her Ellie, please—is a precocious little tweener blessed with a ratty wryness that puts her at odds with her purposeful mother, whose heavenly vision of what her daughter should be bears no resemblance whatever to what Ellie sees for herself. When hostilities reach epic proportions, Ellie packs up and leaves, an act of rebellion and defiance that brings her, kicking and screaming, into the neighborhood of grace. Jerry Camery-Hoggatt's charming Christmas fable is proof that a less-than-accommodating Bethlehem stable still has room for every last one of us."

—DR. JAMES CALVIN SCHAAP, department of English, Dordt College, author of *Startling Joy* and *Romey's Place*

My
Mother's Wish

My Mother's Wish

An American Christmas Carol

Jerry Camery-Hoggatt
author of *When Mother Was Eleven-Foot-Four*

WATERBROOK
PRESS

MY MOTHER'S WISH
PUBLISHED BY WATERBROOK PRESS
12265 Oracle Boulevard, Suite 200
Colorado Springs, Colorado 80921
A division of Random House Inc.

ISBN 978-1-4000-7405-1

Published in the United States by WaterBrook Multnomah, an imprint of The
Doubleday Publishing Group, a division of Random House Inc., New York.

WATERBROOK and its deer colophon are registered trademarks of Random House Inc.

Library of Congress Cataloging-in-Publication Data
Camery-Hoggatt, Jerry.
    My mother's wish : an American Christmas carol / Jerry Camery-Hoggatt.—1st ed.
        p. cm.
    ISBN 978-1-4000-7405-1
    1. Mothers and daughters—Fiction. 2. Christmas stories. I. Title.
PS3603.A454M9 2008
813'.6—dc22

                            2008013290

Printed in the United States of America
2008—First Edition

10 9 8 7 6 5 4 3 2 1

Contrariwise

THE SPANISH POET JUAN RAMÓN JIMÉNEZ ONCE said that if they give you ruled paper, you should write the other way. That's pretty much the story of my life, writing the other way, across the lines, against the grain. I mean this literally. I write my grocery list sideways on the page. I sign my name, Ellee, on the upslope, diagonally across the little boxes they give you on official forms. Ever since the third grade, I've written out my Christmas wish list sideways, running the words up from the bottom, against the grain of the lined paper my mother posts on the refrigerator door. I also write my life story across the lines. I mean this literally too. I write my diary from back to front, too. I hold the book so the pages open from the bottom up, but because I write from back to front, you have to read contrariwise.

A fine word, *contrariwise*. Rolls off the tongue like a marble. It's the best word I know.

I learned it in the seventh grade. I was sitting with my older sister, Susan, next to the entrance to the boys' locker room, watching the rest of the student body mill around like a herd of wildebeests, when that stupid Joey Tyndale rushed up and tried to kiss her. I learned later that he had been taking a dare—things like that happened sometimes to Susie because she's so much prettier than I am—but at the time I didn't know that. Susie almost died of course because Joey Tyndale is a big, lumbering, stupid boy, and in her desperation to get away she knocked my backpack off the bench, and my diary fell out, faceup, on the cracked blacktop of the basketball court.

Miss Buttram, the vice principal, was there in six seconds flat, her first priority to protect Susie (she would have taken a bullet for Susie, she was such a good girl), but I think the real reason was that Miss Buttram loves a good fight on the school grounds. Miss Buttram doesn't have a husband at home to fight with, so she takes her satisfactions where she finds them—the fighting of seventh graders on the playground of the Woodrow Wilson Junior High School, where she has been vice principal since she was thirteen. Nothing gets a person's vice principal sap flowing like a good playground brawl.

I scrambled for the diary but not before Joey saw it and beat me to it, picking it up and taunting me with it. He danced what he thought was a little jig. It was not. He was too big and lumbering to dance a little anything.

"Eleanor writes backwards! Eleanor writes backwards!"

Joey held the diary high so everybody could see, and I started to jump for it.

"Give it back," I said as forcefully as I could with my teeth gritted so nobody else would hear me.

He held the diary higher.

Susie backed away, afraid of getting into trouble, and the small herd of wildebeests that had crowded around us swallowed her up like the phagocytes Mr. Frazier talked about in seventh grade science. Mr. Frazier lived and breathed phagocytes. Every single spelling test he ever gave had the word *phagocyte* on it.

In the corner of my eye, I could see Miss Buttram checking that Susie had not been hurt. It was like that with Susie. Before each school year, the teachers and playground supervisors at our school had a ceremony where they signed a blood pledge that they wouldn't ever, ever let anything hurt Susie McKutcheon, she was so pretty and good.

I bumped against Joey's body as I jumped for my diary, which was like belly-bumping a large marshmallow with arms. "Give it, Joey!" I bit my lip to keep from crying.

When Miss Buttram had finished checking on Susie, she waded into the herd of wildebeests, using all four of her arms to windmill her way through.

"Joey!" That was all Miss Buttram said. It was enough because she used her megaphone voice, which could be heard more than a quarter of a mile away on the top of the water tower with the name of the our town, BLACKWATER, painted in large block letters on the side.

Joey stopped.

There's a rumor that Miss Buttram trained for the vice principal's job by doing a stint with the Green Berets, but I don't believe it. The Green Berets still exist, and they still fight, and that wouldn't be true if Miss Buttram had crossed their path. She would have put a stop to *that* too. I can easily picture her windmilling Green Berets left and right, all four arms in action. So maybe the rumor was true. She clomped around the school in saddle oxfords because they were the closest thing she could find to combat boots.

Joey held the book high, beyond my reach.

"Give. Me. The. Book," Miss Buttram said.

He handed it to her, reaching past me, over my head, to do it.

"Please, Miss Buttram," I said. "It's my diary. It's private."

"Joey. Tyndale. Wait. For. Me. In. My. Office," she said. At Teacher College she had learned to speak in one-word sentences. For her it was a practiced art form, a kind of vice principal's cement poetry. Literally. The words came out in cement. One of them fell on Joey's foot, and he limped away, whimpering.

She began turning the pages of the book, slowly examining them one at a time as though it were the Book of Life. She wondered, I'm sure, if her name was written therein. It was not.

"Please, Miss Buttram…" I said.

"You really do write backward, Eleanor," Miss Buttram said. "Why do you do that?"

"Ellee," I corrected. Then I said, "It's private," to answer her question. It was a partial answer. Writing your diary across the lines seems to me to be an act of self-preservation. I am a pledged disciple of Rosa Parks, a Full Gospel Suffragette. There was a long pause as she examined the pages. The wildebeests lost interest and drifted away, looking for grass. "It's my diary," I said again. "A person has rights."

"Not on my campus," she snapped. She moved her lips, trying to read her way past the puzzling secret backward organization of the diary.

"Leonardo da Vinci wrote backward," I said.

"Not on my campus," Miss Buttram said again. Honestly, you'd think a Green Beret would understand why people write in code sometimes. "You do everything that way," she said.

"What way?" I asked.

"Contrariwise, Eleanor," she said flatly.

The word was wonderful. *Contrariwise.* As it came out of her mouth it took wings. I was so startled I almost gave up on the diary. But not my name. "Ellee," I corrected. Then, "Can I have my diary back, Miss Buttram?"

She handed me the book. "There's a right way to do everything, Eleanor, and a wrong way. You always choose the wrong way."

Eleanor Crumb

B Y NOW YOU SHOULD HAVE GUESSED TWO THINGS. First, that the grownups in my life think my name is Eleanor, which is understandable and forgivable because I couldn't talk when I was born so they had to guess. When the nurse came into my mother's hospital room to fill out my birth certificate, my mother got confused and told the woman I was my grandmother, Eleanor Crumb. The nurse raised an eyebrow at the middle name, Crumb. My mother cocked the hammer of her service revolver and the nurse wrote down "Eleanor Crumb McKutcheon." I don't mind the middle name. It's how I feel a lot of the time. But even if nobody else in the whole world knows my first name is Ellee, I do.

The second thing you should have guessed by now is that when it comes to my name, the grownups aren't very good listeners. I think my mother must have been embarrassed at having reversed our roles, mother and daughter, because she's covered for it ever since. I never met my grandmother—she died the month before I was born—but my father told me once that she wore pearls when she went to the grocery store. I don't even own pearls. My mother covers her embarrassment at the brain glitch by insisting that everybody call me Eleanor.

"If I wanted you to be called Ellee, I would have named you Ellee," she said to me.

She never listens. You'd think a person would know her own name.

Now, my father's a whole other thing altogether. My father calls me by a variety of names, usually whatever vegetable he happens to be thinking about at the time. "Hand me that wrench, will you, Dill Pickle?" Then in a fine imitation of W. C. Fields he would say, "Ah, yes, my little Kumquat…" or "Ah, yes, my little Cucumber…" He told me once his W. C. Fields voice was so good that Hollywood had tried to sign him for silent movies.

"You're a cucumber too," I said to him when I was maybe five.

"The tomato doesn't fall far from the vine," my father replied. Then he called me Tomato for a month.

When he took us with him to kids-and-dads-at-work day, he introduced us to his boss as his daughters, the pride of his life, Susan and Rutabaga. My father spent that night in his recliner.

Miss Buttram calls me Eleanor because my mother visited the school and told her to. When my mother arrived at the school for our intake interview, everybody expected the Clash of the Titans. The school secretary was a mousy-haired woman who wore the uniform of a prison guard. She made my mother write our names on a clipboard, mine and Susie's, and led the three of us down the corridor to the vice principal's office, and I thought I heard her whisper, "Dead man walking," as we passed the little openings where the guidance counselors worked. A panicky-looking janitor came by and unlocked their leg irons, and they quietly left the building on urgent errands in other places. I heard later that Mr. Bartolomeo actually had his class doing duck-and-cover drills, and the English teacher, Miss Houghtalin, took hers to the gymnasium because its walls had steel-reinforced beams that could withstand an atomic blast.

The three of us waited in the dirty oak school chairs Miss Buttram had put outside her office for bad kids, and as we sat, I watched my mother's blood slow-boil at having been kept waiting. Miss Buttram routinely made new parents simmer for exactly thirty-three minutes, stewing in their juices, to make sure they knew whose school it was. I wondered what I should do if my mother and Miss Buttram did battle. I could dive beneath Miss Buttram's steel desk. Susie was on her own.

It never came. The battle I mean. My mother and Miss Buttram turned out to be cut from the same bolt of 30-gauge camouflage. They sat down there and worked out their differences like two Russian politicians cutting a back-room deal to divide Eastern Europe between them. I didn't catch most of what they said. I don't speak Russian. But I knew they had struck a deal when Miss Buttram slapped her fist down hard on the table and said suddenly, "Done!"

After that, at Woodrow Wilson Junior High School I was called Eleanor.

The Pact

THE ONLY TEACHER I EVER HAD WHO DIDN'T break beneath my mother's Iron Will was Mrs. Kate Hathaway, who taught third grade at the elementary school in the shadow of the town water tower. She didn't break, but she bent.

Mrs. Hathaway was a tall, pretty, comfortable woman, with a slow Texas honey-drawl. She wore her hair long, brushed back in a loose ponytail that was tied with a red silk bandanna at the nape of her neck. Fine tendrils of free hair circled her face like a halo. My mother told my father once that she was a "bohemian," I think because she dressed in longish, loose layers of cloth, free-flowing around her body. I thought she looked like a gypsy, minus the bangles. Mr. Davis, the principal, never would have tolerated bangles.

Mrs. Hathaway had a wall where she put framed photographs of the kids in her class, all thirty-seven of us, with our names printed underneath. She printed in elementary-schoolteacher handwriting, with simple lines, but without the cutesy bubbles at the ends of each pen stroke. Beneath my picture, the name said ELEANOR McKUTCHEON. The folded cardboard pup tent on my desk said ELEANOR.

I remember the first day of school because Mrs. Hathaway sat in the front of the room in an oak rocker and called out our names contrariwise, backward, in reverse alphabetical order. She did this, she explained, because all our lives we would hear them read the other way, and in her classroom at least, people with names at the end of the alphabet like Yancey and Zeligman would get a break from having to wait. "Besides," she said, "everybody knows the third-grade alphabet begins with the letter *Z*." The rest of us could "adjust," she said, "in the interests of fair play."

So the names came.

"Zeligman, Alice."

"Here." Zeligman Alice raised her hand.

"Yancey, Thomas."

"Here."

Tyndale Joseph wriggled in his seat in anticipation.

"Tyndale, Joseph."

"Here, Mrs. Hathaway," he said, throwing his hand up

with such force that he knocked his pencil case into Zeligman Alice's lap.

"Thank you, Joseph," Mrs. Hathaway said.

Joey kept his hand up.

"Thank you, Joseph," she said again. "I see your hand."

Knowles Nathan whispered something like, "and I raise you double," which made the boys laugh. We settled down, and the march of names continued.

"Stephenson, John."

"Here."

"Muldoon, Carolyn."

Mrs. Hathaway came to me: "McKutcheon, Eleanor."

"Ellee," I corrected.

Mrs. Hathaway looked at me.

"My name is Ellee," I said. I spelled it for her: "E-L-L-E-E." Then for emphasis I added, "Not Eleanor."

"As you wish," Mrs. Hathaway said. She made a note on her paper with a pencil before continuing down the list.

The next morning when we started school, I was surprised to see that the name beneath my photograph had been changed to ELLEE MCKUTCHEON. The pup tent on my desk read simply ELLEE.

They stayed that way until back-to-school night, when

my mother visited our classroom for the first time. She asked Mrs. Hathaway if they could talk outside. They disappeared for a week. When they came back, Mrs. Hathaway looked at me, a little sadly I remember, but she didn't say anything.

The next morning all the photographs had been taken off the wall, and the pup tent on my desk read ELEANOR. I didn't know where to sit. I felt like something had been taken from me, my home maybe, like I had arrived at school to find all my stuff in a box by the door. My mother had gotten to Mrs. Hathaway.

Mrs. Hathaway came over to me and put her arm around my shoulder and whispered, "Just use your grandmother's desk for now, okay?" So I did, seduced, reluctantly, by the hug and the warmth of her honey-drawl.

Usually, for the two years just before recess, we paired up the way the fifth graders did when they learned to square-dance (a necessary skill for later life), and we drilled each other on the multiplication tables, but since there were an odd number of us Mrs. Hathaway always joined in, rotating which student she drilled. It was her way of checking our progress. This morning she paired with me, asking me to stand beside the steel desk at the back of the room. "Your mother told me about your name," she said quietly.

"It's Ellee," I said. "Not Eleanor."

"She insisted," Mrs. Hathaway said. She didn't have to tell me what my mother had said next—"If I wanted the girl to be called Ellee, I would have named her Ellee"—but Mrs. Hathaway added gently, "She said it was your grandmother's name."

"My grandmother died before I was born," I said. "I'm pretty sure I'm not her."

Mrs. Hathaway leaned in conspiratorially close. "Listen, Ellee," she said quietly. "Do you know what it is to reach a compromise?"

I shook my head.

"It's finding a way to play the game so everybody wins."

"Like T-ball," I said.

She nodded. "Like T-ball. You give a little and I give a little, and we both come out all right. Does that make sense?"

"So what do you want me to do?" I asked.

She lowered her voice. "I know for a hard fact that the desk belonged to your grandmother."

"How do you know that?" I asked.

"I had my husband break into your house last night and steal it from your family's plunder room." I must have looked puzzled, because she paused in her little tale. "In Texas, a plunder room is what you-all call an attic. We won't tell anybody about that though, you understand. I need you to sit in it to keep it safe."

I steeled for the worst. "You gonna call me Eleanor now?"

"No, of course not," Mrs. Hathaway said to me then. "Between us, I'll call you by your real name. Ellee. When your mother visits, I'll call you Miss McKutcheon."

I listened to this, unconvinced that everybody would win. I had no bargaining chips to lay on the table.

"And just between us, you know, just the two of us, you may call me Kate. With everybody else you'll have to call me Mrs. Hathaway."

I whispered, "Done!"

She gave me one of those sideways teacher hugs, which sealed the deal. It sealed something else between us, but I didn't realize that until much, much later.

A Gypsy's Dream

MRS. HATHAWAY MOVED AWAY TO NEBRASKA the year I started high school, and I never saw her again, not in "hard fact," as she might say. But I did see her in a dream. In the dream I was sixteen, a junior at some high school I saw in *Seventeen* magazine in an article called "The High School of the Future—Are You Ready?" Mrs. Hathaway's third-grade classroom was there in the middle of the school, only instead of four walls it was a circle of wagons, a gypsy camp. The wagons were circled, I realized, to create a protective barrier, to keep her hoard of children from having to grow up too fast.

That's the teacher's dilemma, I thought in my dream, *to get their children ready for the "High School of the Future" and at the same time make a protected hideout where they can still be children.* Mrs. Hathaway's hideout was a gypsy camp.

She was sitting in the same oak rocker, stirring a black cauldron of steaming goulash over an open fire.

"Miss McKutcheon!" she said when she saw me, and then, more softly, "Ellee." She rocked forward, launching herself into a full standing position. She was smaller than I remembered, or I was taller, because now we were talking head to head, standing up. She held me out at arm's length, "Let me look at you."

I submitted to this inspection a little self-consciously because I was sixteen and gangly, but I did it because it allowed me to look at her too. She looked just the same, except that now over her loose, layered clothing, she wore the bangles Mr. Davis would not have permitted—two or three chains of gold coins around her neck and another larger one low on her hips.

"I came to say thank you," I said.

"Why, Ellee, whatever for?" she asked. I looked around the camp. Our pictures were there, hanging on the side of one of the wagons, all thirty-seven of us, except that the pictures depicted us as she imagined us to be, all grown up. High school graduation portraits of our best selves. Joey Tyndale was actually handsome. I checked the name again. Tyndale. Whodathunkit? The boy was handsome. That was how I knew this was a dream. Our names were printed underneath our pictures. Mine said ELLEE McKUTCHEON.

"For that," I said, indicating the picture. "For calling me by my name."

"Let me tell you a secret," she said. She gestured to a log on the other side of the fire, and I sat down. She sat back in the rocker. As she moved, the gold from the coins caught the firelight and turned into strings of fireflies around her neck and waist. "You want some of this goulash?" she asked.

I shook my head. "No, thank you."

"The name on my birth certificate is Cecily," she said. She sipped at the goulash from a golden spoon, caught her breath at the fiery spices, and choked on the heat.

"Cecily?" I said.

"Hot," she gasped, waving her hand in front of the goulash.

I found some water in an open barrel, located the ladle, and fished her out a drink.

She whispered, still choking, "My mother thought Cecily was the grandest name she had ever heard." Then she sat silent for a long time, rocking and catching her breath. Finally she said, "Cecily Lenore. She named me that because it symbolized all her best dreams for me. That I might turn into a grand lady, a politician's wife maybe, or maybe the Grand Dame of the Ladies' Sewing Circle. My mother was big on sewing circles. And high tea." She tried the goulash again, sipping more respectfully this time.

"I thought your first name was Kate," I said.

She lifted one eye and looked at me. "Do I look like a Cecily to you?"

A long pause. I didn't know what to say to that. That was when I realized that something very deep had been sealed between us. I couldn't guess what to call it, but it will be with me until the day I die. I rose to leave. "Thank you again, Mrs. Hathaway."

"Ellee," she said softly. She reached back and drew her gypsy shawl close around her shoulders. "It's your dream," she said, "and I wouldn't want to tell you how to run it, but I sure as thunder hope you didn't let Mr. Davis in here. I'd be pleased if you'd just call me Kate."

The fire flickered out, and the fireflies turned back into gold coins. Mrs. Hathaway disappeared. The wagons disappeared. The "School of the Future" disappeared. I drifted into a deeper sleep.

When I woke up, I realized that I had forgotten to

thank Mrs. Kate Hathaway for something else. She was the one who told me about Juan Ramón Jiménez. If they give you ruled paper, write the other way. Mrs. Hathaway was the reason I write my Christmas list sideways, from the bottom up.

Mother's Wish

THE FIRST DAY OF DECEMBER EVERY YEAR, MY mother posts four folded sheets of lined notebook paper on the refrigerator door, with our names written on top. MOM. DAD. SUSAN. ELEANOR. We're supposed to list the things we really really want for Christmas so the gift giving will be correct and efficient. I always found that odd. In my view, the point of choosing presents is to get to know the other person so well that you don't have to be told what she really really wants for Christmas. You just know it. If somebody gives you something you don't like, like a puce sweater or a Nehru jacket with gold trim…well, that just tells you something, doesn't it?

But with this, like everything else, my mother insisted. I learned the hard way. If I didn't write anything on the list, she gave me "things intended for Eleanor." Fine bone china.

Silver hand mirrors. Puce-colored cashmere sweaters with little gems glued onto the bodice in a floral pattern.

So I learned to put down what I wanted as a way of protecting myself. If I didn't, the rest of my life she would want to know why I never wore my puce sweater. But I wrote my stupid Christmas wish list contrariwise, across the grain, turning the page so the words ran up from the bottom. Once I wrote "a gypsy dress," but that never came, I think because my mother couldn't picture "her Eleanor" in a gypsy dress. People see what they want to see.

When I was eleven, my mother told me I had to rewrite the entire list "properly, *with* the lines, as a good girl should" before she would let me open a single present. "Susie never does stupid stuff like that," she said.

The presents waited until my birthday in March.

Susie never did stupid stuff like I did. She always wrote *with* the lines, and she always put down good girl things like bone china, tortoiseshell combs for her hair, collectible dolls, and pearls.

My father always put "horehound drops" because they tasted so bitter and awful he knew they were the only candy he wouldn't have to share with his children. "It's a question of territory," he said.

"What's *territory* got to do with horehound drops?" I asked.

"Ask Miss Buttram," my father said.

For as long as I can remember, my mother's own Christmas wish list had a practical bent to it. In a beautiful, fluid hand, she wrote things like "new washing machine" or "curlers." Curlers were big in those days, in both meanings of that term. They were great big monstrous things she attached to her head so she could receive daily radio updates from the mother ship. Everybody did. They wrapped them in toilet paper to improve reception. One year my mother asked for clear plastic seat covers for the DeSoto and a Trinitron television set so we could watch Ed Sullivan in living color. She wanted the plastic seat covers because they would protect the seats from sweat stains and keep them nice for resale. My father said that plastic seat covers were what made you sweat in the first place, and what's wrong with the seats being nice for *us* right now, for Pete's sake? The world is divided into these two camps.

Mother had to wait for the washing machine too, because my father ignored the list and gave her what she really really wanted: a cashmere sweater with glued-on floral-pattern gems and a pink silk Nehru jacket because it was all the rage. When my mother wore it, she turned into Madame Chiang Kai-shek and ruled our house the way the Iron Lady ruled China.

I knew too that there were other things she really really wanted and never wrote down on her Christmas wish list, things that were far closer to her heart than cashmere sweaters and Nehru jackets. She wished my father would speak up for himself and demand a promotion at work. She wished he would let her replace the olive-drab recliner in the front room where he read the paper. ("It's ugly," he insisted, "but it's a question of territory." He was right about that. Sometimes when I was little, I would climb up there and fall asleep on his lap. It was an island of my father surrounded by a sea of my mother.)

My mother had wishes for me too. She wished that I would run for office at the high school, like Susie did. "It'll help you meet a nice young man don't you think it's about time?" she said. She wished that I would take up with a better crowd, like Susie's friends. She wished that I would work harder in school, like Susie.

She wished that I was Eleanor.

The Gold Standard

THE KICKER CAME TWO WEEKS AFTER SUSIE married Jim Darling. I forget his real name. He was perfectly coiffed. Perfectly behaved. He wore a white shirt and tie the day he came to pick Susie up for their first date. He addressed my mother as "Mrs. McKutcheon" and said "yes, ma'am" no matter what she asked. He had no personality at all, not that I could see. A perfectly manicured, perfectly coiffed dishrag. He was perfect to a fault. After he and Susie got married, they took a job posing for photographs on the tops of wedding cakes.

The wedding was a disaster. Everything worked according to a precise plan, including me, because my mother threatened me with the AK-47 Miss Buttram had sold her out of the trunk of her car. "It's Susie's day," she said to me, brandishing the rifle, but I put up no fuss because she was right, of course. On this one day, I was a good child too.

Susie asked me to be her maid of honor, which I think she did because my mother insisted it was the right thing to do.

"You'll look so pretty in the photographs, you and Eleanor," Mother said.

What she meant was that Susie would look prettier standing next to me. Photographic foils. Dr. Jekyll looks so much better posing next to Mr. Hyde. I was a prop, for Pete's sake.

We stood at the back of the Blackwater Baptist Church, waiting for the music to pause so we could make our grand entrance. We were wearing the kind of brides-maid dresses that are specifically designed to make the bride look good by contrast. More photographic foils. For his groomsmen, Jim Darling brought in the Lost Boys and dressed them up like penguins; they came in varying height, weight, and hair length. I was paired with his best friend, a tall, gangling man-boy named Elwood or Elbow, something like that. He was perfectly forgettable, except that he was wearing his father's tuxedo, which was too short for him so yards and yards of arm stuck out of the ends of the sleeves like tree limbs.

My mother hovered over us like a monarch butterfly,

fluttering in to give directions, then drifting out again to bask in her royal butterfly glory. "A little straighter there, Eleanor," she said to me. "You're so pretty when you stand up straight." Just before Eldon-the-man-boy-of-the-tree-limb-arms came to escort her to the mother-of-the-bride seat, she turned to me, touched her shoulder holster, and said, from behind a ventriloquist's smile, "If you know what's good for you, you'll make sure you don't trip on anything." She allowed the smile to blossom for the on-lookers and fluttered up to give us all a final inspection. Then she dropped down again, placed her arm on a knot of Elrod's left limb, and processed into the church like Catherine the Great on coronation day.

In the end, Susie had her clockwork wedding. At pre-cisely forty-three minutes after two, we left the church for the reception, with white folding chairs set out on the grass beneath the small sea of umbrellas the men of the church had set up. Victorian Missouri. It was a picture perfect July day, as my mother had instructed in her prayers. A clear, stunning blue sky. Slight breeze. At a signal from my mother, the birds lined up and flew in formation to honor Mr. and Mrs. Darling as they left the church. The tulips beside the walk bowed low and sang a little song as the happy couple passed, and for a moment Susie was the Good Witch of the North, blessing Munchkins.

The single unplanned moment was when Joey Tyndale threw puffed rice to suggest that Susie might be pregnant. Nobody noticed but me. Apparently he either didn't know or didn't care that beneath her lace shawl my mother was packing heat.

Either way, I loved him for that.

Otherwise the clockwork wedding was perfect, but how could it not be? The gods of chaos had had eighteen years to learn that on Susan McKutcheon's wedding day they'd better not cross my mother or they would be demoted to demigods and banished from the garden of delights. Her prewedding prayer had been an exorcism: "Gods of chaos, begone!" And they had shuddered and stammered back, "Yes, Mrs. McKutcheon," and trundled off to Tahlequah.

"Smile, Eleanor," my mother said as we stood together in the reception line. "You have such a pretty smile." What she meant was that my smile pointed outward to my ears, which my mother thought were my very best feature. Was the woman blind? I was smiling fast. A string came up from behind my jaw and through a little hole in the top of my head, where it joined with other strings tied to my hands and feet. I was nodding my head and smiling and dancing a little marionette dance and saying, "No, I'm not next," and "How good of you to come," and "No, I'm not next."

I wanted to run, but the strings wouldn't have reached the property line. I was admiring Mrs. Homer Johnson's perfectly ghastly hat and saying, "How good of you to come," when I got a picture in my head of running away from home when I was six years old. I had put a peanut butter sandwich in a handkerchief and tied it on the end of a pole and headed out the door. I was Opie, looking for Mayberry.

I stopped to tell my father I was going.

He looked up from his paper. "Write to me from college," he said.

"Aren't you going to drive me?" I asked.

He set down the paper and came over to me. He squatted down so we could see eye to eye, placed his hand on the top of my head, and turned my face toward his. "I've got a better idea, Kumquat," he said. "I'll blow you up like a balloon and you can float there." He tackled me and rolled me over and over on the carpet, and then he put his face into my stomach and blew so hard I actually did fill up and float toward the ceiling.

We stopped when my mother came in. She was wearing her bathrobe and curlers, and her face was covered with Pond's cold cream. When we went out for a fine supper at Chitlins, she wore pearls and puce. When we were home, she wore curlers and cold cream.

"She can't go to college today," she said.

"And why not?" my father asked. "She's ready." He indicated the sandwich on the pole. Then he pulled on an imaginary string, hauling me down from the ceiling.

"She has to clean her room," my mother said.

She reached out and took the string from my father. (I think now, reflecting back, that it was the very same string she used to keep me smiling at my sister's wedding to Jim Darling.)

My father winked at me and said he had his own reason why I couldn't run away to college when I was only six years old.

"Why not?" I asked.

"Because I'd have to wait up for you, and I can't stay awake that long."

WHEN MRS. HOMER JOHNSON SAID SOMETHING LIKE, "Have you met my grandson, Eldridge?" the string pulled hard, and I smiled and said, "Why, no, Mrs. Johnson." And she said, "I'd like for you to come to supper sometime." The string pulled, and I said, "I'd like that, Mrs. Johnson."

I was smiling so hard my teeth hurt. Maybe my teeth hurt because they were gritted. It's hard to smile through gritted teeth. How could I smile when my sister had just married a dishrag? It wasn't a question of whether I loved my sister—which I did. I wasn't smiling because Jim Darling was now the Gold Standard against which every boy I ever dated would be measured.

"He's such a *catch*!" my mother's friends had said over tea when she told them about the engagement. My mother beamed. He really was a catch. My mother and Susie had reeled him in like a fish, which wasn't hard because dishrags don't put up any fight. My mother had even weighed him on a hanging scale and measured his length. If he struggled now, after this, my mother would have him for breakfast.

It was hard to smile because I knew that once Susie was married off, I really would be "next." Finding a boy who measured up to Jim Darling would become my mother's full-time project. She made checklists, for Pete's sake.

"Gods of chaos, come back," I whispered in my heart of hearts. It was hard to smile because I was imagining who my mother would catch for me. I crossed myself—an unexpected Catholic—and whispered a prayer for Elroy, who was, thankfully, homing in on Zeligman Alice. In long twig fingers, he held two crystal punch cups like birds' nests. He smiled. She smiled. Alfalfa and Darla. For the moment I was safe.

Precisely

TWO WEEKS AFTER SUSIE'S WEDDING, THE HAPPY couple came back happier from their honeymoon, and my mother threw a little welcome home tea for them. After the tea, when Susie and her friends had gone back to Neverland, I cleared the table while my mother covered the leftovers and put them in the refrigerator. My father ran hot water into the sink, getting ready to wash the china, which my mother insisted had to be done by hand because the new Sears and Roebuck automatic dishwasher didn't know anything about china.

I watched his reflection in the window as I came back with the last of the dishes. My father is a good man, a quiet, unassuming man who seldom asks anything for himself beyond horehound drops. He lives his life, it can be said, in my mother's wake. I set the dishes down on the counter next to the sink and picked up a dishtowel.

"You don't have to do that, my little Kumquat," he said to me in his best W. C. Fields voice. "Don't you have homework to do?"

"Not in July," I said. But he stole the dishtowel and tried to snap me with it, chasing me from the room. I went upstairs and put on my pajamas and bathrobe. I was coming back to help put away the china when I was stopped dead in my tracks in the hall. In the kitchen, on the other side of the wall, my father and mother were arguing.

"She's incorrigible," my mother was saying, "and you encourage her."

"Like how?" my father said.

"Like calling her those stupid vegetable names." I heard what might have been a sob, but I couldn't be sure because Iron Ladies don't sob. It makes their cheeks rust.

"I'm not going to call her Eleanor," my father said. "She hates the name Eleanor."

"Eleanor was my mother's name," she said indignantly.

"Precisely!" my father said. "Ellee's not your mother. She's herself. She's sweet, and I'm proud of her." I could hear china clink hard against china as he dried what must have been the last of the plates. The clinks were getting louder, more forceful.

"Herself!" my mother groaned. "Herself? She thinks she's a bohemian. No. No. What's the word? She thinks she's a gypsy." She raised her voice on that last word— gypsy—for emphasis: "She thinks she's a *gypsy*."

"Keep your voice down," he ordered. "She'll hear you."

I heard my mother's voice again, lower this time. "She's turning out all wrong, John. She's a tramp."

For the first time I can remember, my father's voice went steely too. What he said he said one word at a time: "You. Will. Not. Say. Such. Things. About. My. Daughter." The words came out in cement, and each one shattered another china plate as they crashed one at a time on the table. They…were…spaced…shattering…exclamation points.

By this time my mother was sobbing outright. It had been my grandmother's best bone china.

This, it turned out, was the Clash of the Titans, the battle I had always dreaded, but surprisingly I felt something toward my father I had never felt before. I was proud of him. My father was doing battle. For a brief moment I wondered if I should be looking for a place to hide beneath Miss Buttram's steel desk.

Instead I went up to my room and changed into my

street clothes. By this time I was crying too. I was proud of my father but so, so sorry to have disappointed my mother the way I had. "I'm sorry, Grandmother Crumb," I whispered, "but I just can't wear pearls."

I emptied the books from my backpack and stuck in a toothbrush, a pair of jeans, a sweatshirt, a change of underwear. I slipped into my parents' room and scooped up a handful of horehound drops, each one a bittersweet talisman of my father. I went back to my room, took out a piece of notebook paper, and wrote a note to my father, which I folded and stuck in a pocket of my jeans. I left the house the way Romeo left Juliet, climbing out the window and down the trellis and away.

Before I hit the highway, I stopped at my father's DeSoto, which was parked in the driveway. The driver's side front window was cracked to let in air. I slipped the note in through the crack and watched it lodge itself beside the driver's seat. I had written, "I love you, Daddy. I'm sorry. It's not your fault. Don't wait up. I'll write to you from college. Always Ellee." Next to my name, in parentheses, I added, "Kumquat."

The Comeback Café

S O THAT'S HOW I ENDED UP IN THE WAITING AREA OF the Comeback Truck-Stop Café thirty miles outside of Hastings with no money and no prospects and an empty space in my stomach the size of the Cooper County grain elevator. It's winter, and I'm sitting out a storm in the waiting area, trying hard not to be noticed by the waitress, who is a big, rawboned, heavyset woman with three arms. Two of the arms hold plates of food; the third holds a steel coffeepot. She sees me anyway.

"What you doin' in here, honey?" she asks. Her face is a wrinkled road map of a life that must have been a hard, hard journey.

"I'm waiting out the storm," I said quietly.

"You hungry?" the waitress said.

"Is it all right if I just stay here a while until the rain lets up?"

"Suit yourself," she said. Her face softened, and I could see that she must have been pretty once. *Pretty* the way my mother defined pretty. She slipped a plate down in front of a Weary Traveler, and one of the arms disappeared. I wondered for a moment about the journey that had led her to this place, the journey that had pressed those lines on a pretty face.

She turned to somebody who must have been one of the truckdrivers. "Come on, Jedidiah, your table's ready." He had been studying a Rand McNally road map of the Midwest. He stood up, folded the map and put it into the pocket of a leather jacket, looked down at me, and said, "Come on, kid. It's on me. I hate to eat alone."

I followed him into the dining room, which was packed with flotsam and jetsam that had been washed up by the storm. A solid wall of Big Men was seated on stools at the linoleum counter. You couldn't tell them apart because they wore identical farmer uniforms with identical green John Deere caps, and they lived interchangeable lives. They were pistons in the same machine. Before them, in various stages of consumption, sat their identical suppers of chicken-fried steak. And plastic drinking glasses filled with thick brown gravy because in the Midwest, gravy is a beverage.

Beneath a careworn Christmas tree in the corner was a pile of empty boxes wrapped in tired red-and-white-striped paper. They looked like convicts sitting there, and I guessed they'd been locked away in some storage unit year in and year out, punctuated by an annual month of parole at Christmastime.

A different waitress in a stained apron slapped down somebody's blue-plate special, and when the man dug into it, a cloud of steam the size and shape of the plume at Nagasaki filled the room. I shuddered and looked away. The man's children would all be mutants.

In a booth in the corner, a young mother was trying to quiet a screaming baby. The baby was screaming because it couldn't get its gravy to come out of the nipple of its baby bottle—poor thing. Poor mother—the baby had Miss Buttram's lungs. A chrome-plated nickel jukebox on one of the tables was belting out Christmas carols. I was trapped in one of those Christmas stories that gives schmaltz a bad name.

One of the Big Men stood up to help the woman with the baby, an old man whose face was half-burned, the way farmers and construction workers get from wearing hats to protect their eyes from the sun. The top half was creamy white like the mashed potatoes on his plate. The lower half was as red as baked beans. The hair sticking out from beneath his cap was snow white. A grandfather. Even against the backdrop of schmaltz, it was a touching thing to see, the way this tender giant coddled that little baby girl. He sang a lullaby, but at first I couldn't hear what it was over the clatter of Melmac dishes and the constant jarring sound of silverware being slammed into steel racks in the dish room behind the wall.

After a long moment the baby was sleeping, sucking a tiny thumb, drawing comfort from her inner self. That sight alone was worth the exile from my father and mother. Someone turned down the volume of the background noise, and I began to make out what the old man was singing.

> Lully, lullay, Thou little tiny Child,
> By, by, lully, lullay.
> Lully, lullay, Thou little tiny Child,
> By, by, lully, lullay.

He had a fine baritone voice, singing us all softly into calm.

Yikes! I thought. *The schmaltz is thicker than the gravy.*

When he changed to a medieval folk carol, the dish-washers in the back room stopped slamming dishes into washing racks. The lyric ended with

> With song she lullèd him asleep
> That was so sweet a melody
> It passèd alle minstrelsy....

What manner of man is this, I thought to myself, *that he weareth the raiment of a tiller of the soil and yet knoweth such sweet minstrelsy as this?*

Grandfather began moving slowly through the restaurant, a warm, rich baritone rendition of "Silent Night" ebbing from him like the balm-of-Gilead. He did not sing this in English, but in German, *"Stille Nacht, Heilige Nacht...."* He still held the sleeping baby. He was completely indifferent to the rest of us; he neither knew nor cared that we were there. In a very real sense, the baby held him as firmly as he held her.

And in the same way that the baby held him, he held us. As long as Grandfather held us under his spell, the bus-boy couldn't bus, the waitresses couldn't wait, and the manager couldn't manage. His renditions of "Dona Nobis Pacem" and "In Dulci Jubilo" could have charmed snakes. The Big Men set down their gravy glasses and listened. Everything drew down to a hush. He wrapped us in a blanket of holiness. Even the storm outside seemed to subside for a moment, the wind knocked out of it by Grandfather's spell.

He finished off the set with a rendition of Gounod's "Ave Maria" that was so tender it knocked your socks off. When he finished, I wanted to applaud but didn't, because schmaltz or no schmaltz, that old man had made this restaurant into a church by creating a hallowed space within it and, within that hallowed space, a transforming moment. Somehow he had managed to pick us up and coddle us across that whisper-thin line between schmaltz and profundity.

That was when Jedidiah said, "Did you see what I saw?"

I nodded, speechless. It wasn't simply that Grandfather had sung these songs, but that he had had these songs within him to sing, and a voice that could charm snakes with which to sing them. He looked so much like the others that I had thought him ordinary; now I thought that perhaps each of the others might be equally extraordinary in his own way. I looked again along the line of Big Men and was surprised to see that each profile was now absolutely unique; each face bore its own distinctive road map of creases and wrinkles to track its journey. That was the precise moment I realized that they were not merely Farmers and Big Men; they might well be Heroes and Giants, just as my father, John C. Calhoun McKutcheon, is a hero and a giant.

"Well, then," Jedidiah said, "we're done here. It's time to head home."

Home, I thought. *If you only knew.*

Grandfather handed the baby gently down to its mother, and then as quickly as it had come, the moment passed. The Giants went back to their chicken-fried steak; the clatter of knives and forks began again, in workmen's rhythm. Somewhere behind a screen I heard a woman's voice say, "Order up." Outside, the storm caught its breath and kicked up again, released from Grandfather's spell.

One last time I looked along the line of Giants at the counter. There at the far end, Grandfather's face had turned just so in the light, and I saw, perfectly formed against the knotty pine wall, my own fond father's face in profile.

My heart broke and fell out onto the table.

Jedidiah picked it up gently and handed it back to me. "You'll need this," he said.

He diced what was left of his pork loin into tiny pieces and called for a takeout box and the check.

The waitress brought the box but refused the check. "On me," she said simply.

As we left the restaurant, she glanced around, probably watching for the manager, then handed me a white paper bag filled with sandwiches. I paused and looked at her, hard.

"I got me a kid of my own out there somewhere, honey," she said. "Same age as you."

That explained at least the deepest creases of her weathered face. They eased a little as she handed me the bag, and I thought I saw Mrs. Hathaway, or maybe Mrs. Hathaway's sister, still pretty underneath. For a moment, fireflies danced around her pretty face.

"Thank you, Kate," I said.

She looked at me oddly and said, "Kate don't work here no more, honey," and pointed to her name badge, which said, simply, "Nadine."

"Thank you, Nadine," I said. Suddenly it seemed terribly important to me to know her real name. "And what's the old man's name?" I asked, indicating Grandfather.

"Elwood," she said.

"Thank you," I said. "I won't forget that."

If hunger does strange things to a person, so does being fed.

The Good
Ship Horvath

W E STOOD AT THE DOOR, MAPPING THE route to Jedidiah's truck. "You're cold," he said.

"I left my puce sweater at home," I said.

He unzipped his jacket and threw it around my shoulders against the rain. Underneath, he wore an embroidered gypsy's vest. He saw that I saw that he wore this and said simply, "It came with the truck."

I peered at the truck through the sheet rain. On the side of the trailer, in large letters, the company logo said HORVATH, and then beneath that, in smaller letters, DISTRIBUTORS OF FINE GOULASH.

We made a run for it, dodging lightning. "Up you go," he said, offering to help me up the chrome ladder into the passenger's seat of his cab. I threw in my backpack and scrambled up the ladder after it.

A small cat came out from a corner of the cab.

"Another stray?" I asked, as he climbed in on the driver's side. The cat had three good legs and a stiff one. I pictured her as a pirate's cat with a red bandanna, an eyepatch, and a wooden leg. One, two, three, *thump*. One, two, three, *thump*—upon the oaken planking of the lower deck.

"Now don't worry, Cecily," he said to the cat. "She's good people." And then, "She's with me."

Cecily? I thought. *He named his cat Cecily?* I was disappointed in Jedidiah. The cat should have been named Mrs. Smee.

He opened up the pork loin and held it out to her as he introduced us.

I gave him back his jacket.

"I'm headed south toward St. Louis," he said was he settled in at the helm. Mrs. Smee abandoned the pork loin and retreated to her berth below deck.

I saluted. "Aye, aye, Captain." I got a picture of my father's profile against the knotty pine wall of the restaurant, and I almost asked him to drop me off when we got near Blackwater, but then it occurred to me that my mother had probably changed the locks. If she had, I didn't want to know. Instead I said simply, "Permission to remain aboard, sir?"

"Listen," Jedidiah said, "climb up over the back of the seat. There's a bedroll in the sleeper."

I scrambled up to the captain's stateroom, a fine accommodation with little round porthole windows on both starboard and port sides.

He switched on a map light to make an entry in his ship's log: 22:00 HOURS. 30 NAUTICAL MILES S OF HASTINGS, NEBRASKA. WIND: 45 KNOTS SSW. HEAVY RAIN. HEADING: SSE. SUPPLIES LOW. PLENTY GOULASH.

"Go to sleep," he said as he did this. "I'll wake you up in the morning." Then he reached into his jacket pocket and fished out the map of the Midwest he had been studying. He held it under the light. He peered through the window, taking a sighting with a brass sextant.

I looked over his shoulder. "You're lost," I said. I didn't know truckers ever got lost. "So tell me how you got lost."

"What? You writing a book?" He fired up the Good Ship Horvath, hauled anchor, and we motored toward the mouth of the harbor with a deep rumble of the below-deck forward engines. Through the starboard window I could see Nadine the Waitress standing in the light of the doorway. In one hand she held a plate of food for some Weary Traveler, in one her steel coffeepot. With her third arm she wiped away tears. Nadine the Waitress was piping us out to sea; Nadine the Mother was crying.

Just as we passed the door of the restaurant, Jedidiah shifted gears with such force that Mrs. Smee came up over the seat and sought refuge beside me in the bedroll. He pulled out onto the highway, grinding gears as he went. "Old truck," he said.

"Tell me how you got lost," I said again. "Off the record."

He said something like, "There's lots of ways of being lost, kid, and lots…" I didn't hear how this finished because by then I was gone completely, lullèd to sleep by the weariness in my bones, and the food in my belly, and the roar of the engine, and the purr of the cat, and the sweet spicy smell of the goulash in the hold, and the hard slap of the windshield wipers against the heavy rain.

Blackwater

I WOKE UP AS WE ROLLED THROUGH ANOTHER SLEEPY midwestern town, all dark. Even the Christmas lights were turned off, evidence of Midwestern practicality. A hard, bright light somewhere ahead of us said the water tower was still lighted, and I scrambled down into the passenger's seat to try to get a fix on where we were.

"Done sleeping, kid?" Jedidiah asked.

"Ellee," I said. "McKutcheon."

"Short for Eleanor?" he asked.

"Short for Ellee," I said.

"Glad to meet you, Ellee McKutcheon," Jedidiah said. He extended a hand. We shook. His hand was a steel vise.

The dark shape of a grain elevator loomed up on our left as we drove into town. It looked like a rocket ship readying for takeoff. I wished I had my mother's curlers to make contact. "We're in Cape Canaveral," I said, but I knew it wasn't true. The rain had stopped, and in the dim moonlight I had made out the words COOPER COUNTY GROWERS ASSOCIATION painted on the side of the grain elevator. I knew without looking what was painted on the water tower: HOME OF THE TITANS. Above that, in larger letters, BLACKWATER.

Jedidiah laughed out loud when he saw the word *Blackwater* painted on the side of a water tower.

I laughed too. "I've got this picture in my head of the town fathers gathering somewhere deep beneath the Missouri topsoil, shaking their heads that nobody up top gets the joke."

"That tells me a lot about your town," Jedidiah said.

"My father thinks it's a hoot," I said.

"That tells me a lot about you," Jedidiah said.

"The tomato doesn't fall far from the vine," I said.

He revved the engine, downshifted, stopped at a light, and then turned right at the elementary school and right again at the Blackwater Baptist Church. He turned into our neighborhood and dropped anchor in front of my family's bungalow. Our house alone still had its Christmas lights on; the rest of the block was dark. Surprisingly to me, a single bright porch light beamed above the screen door, turning the porch into a lighthouse. He cut engine.

"End of the line," he said. "This is where you get out."

I looked hard at him. "Who are you?" I said. And, "How did you know this is where I live?"

"Like I told you, Ellee, there's lots of ways of being lost and lots of ways of being found." He drummed with his hands on the steering wheel. "You'd better get out now. Go on. Get out before I throw you out."

"Aye, Captain," I said. I saluted, squared my cap, reached for my duffel bag, and got ready to go ashore as soon as the mooring lines were tied off.

"Wait," he said. "There's something more."

I looked at him, curious.

"Be gentle with your mother," he said.

I looked at him, startled.

"Behind the Pond's cold cream, her face, too, is a wrinkled road map of a hard, hard journey," he said.

I looked at him, absolutely dumbfounded.

"She lost her own battle with the real Eleanor Crumb years and years before you were born."

"Who *are* you?" I asked again.

"I told you that too," he said simply. "My name is Jedidiah."

"Where'd you get a name like Jedidiah?"

"It was my mother's grandest hope for me," he said. "It means something like 'Beloved of God.'"

"What's your *full* name, Mr. Jedidiah-Beloved-of-God?" I said.

"Out you go," he said. "Go on, get out of here."

He waited until I was on terra firma, then called out after me, "Captain Jedidiah Hathaway, Master of the Good Ship Horvath, at your service."

I stared at him. "Hathaway?"

"Hathaway," he said again. He winked. "I believe you know my wife."

I looked back when I reached the porch. The Good Ship Horvath had hauled anchor and sailed silently away into the night.

In a Sliver of Light

T HE DOOR WAS UNLOCKED, WHICH UNDER different circumstances I would have chalked up to another Midwestern sensibility, but as I slipped inside I realized that it was unlocked because some night just like this one, I might come home without a key. The porch light was on in my father's hope that I might see it and find my way home, even from as far away as Nebraska.

I knew these things because my father was asleep in his ugly green recliner, which he had positioned so he could see the door. Even after five months, he was still waiting up for Kumquat, sound asleep.

I didn't wake him because I wasn't really sure I could stay, and I didn't want to break his heart a second time. I slipped past him into the kitchen, where I got a glass from the cupboard and cracked the refrigerator door, looking for milk. That was when I saw them, six folded strips of notebook paper stuck on the door with magnets. DAD, MOM, SUSAN, CARL (which was Jim Darling's real name), CARL JR., ELEANOR. Something was wrong with the name ELEANOR, and I took it down and held it where I could read it in the thin sliver of light from the refrigerator door.

The name ELEANOR had been crossed out. Above it, in my mother's hand, written on the upslope, I read my name. ELLEE.

I looked closer. If she had crossed out ELEANOR with a scribble, it would have indicated an act of passion or anger, or worse, a capitulation to her failure as a mother. But the name had been crossed out with a ruler, a single perfectly straight line that began with the letter E and ended with R. An act of decision. A decisive turn.

I reached over and took my mother's list off the refrigerator door and held it up to the light. My hand was trembling, and I had to steady the list against the side of the refrigerator. There was only one entry, written out in my mother's perfect fluid hand:

"All I want is Ellee."

There you have it,

My American Christmas carol.

My three grandest hopes for you are:

That you will know you are Beloved of God,

That if you ever find yourself at the Comeback Café,

God will send Jedidiah Hathaway and the Good Ship Horvath

To find you and carry you home in the night,

And that when you get there

They will serve you goulash and call you by your real name.

With best Christmas wishes,

Eilee Kumquat McCutcheon Tyndale

Gypsy

JERRY CAMERY-HOGGATT, PHD, is Professor of New Testament and Narrative Theology at Vanguard University. He's a professional storyteller and is the author of the Christmas stories *When Mother Was Eleven-Foot-Four: A Christmas Memory* (in both adult and children's picture-book formats) and *Giver of Gifts: Three Stories of Christmas Grace.* He's also the author of *Irony in Mark's Gospel: Text and Subtext, Grapevine: The Spirituality of Gossip,* and *Reading the Good Book Well: A Guide to Biblical Interpretation.* As a narrative theologian, he takes special joy in discovering the ways God complicates our plots in artful plays to turn us into more interesting and Christlike characters.